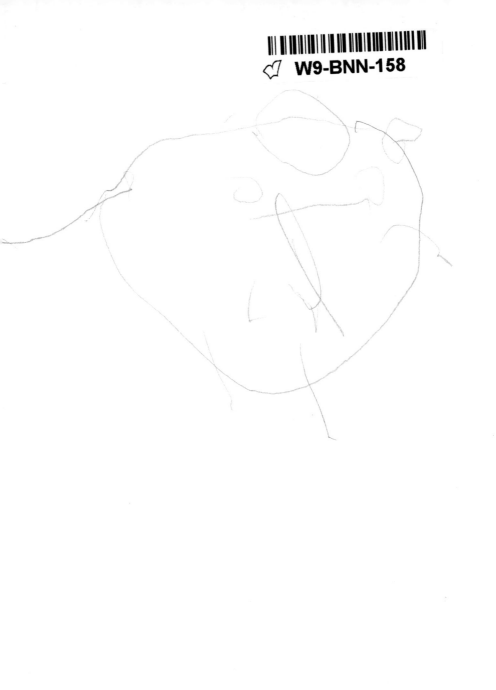

Rescue at Sea!

Rescue at Sea!

By Wolfram Hänel

Illustrated by Ulrike Heyne

Translated by Rosemary Lanning

North-South Books
New York / London

First published in the United States, Great Britain, Canada,
Australia, and New Zealand in 1999 by North-South Books,
an imprint of Nord-Süd Verlag AG, Gossau Zürich, Switzerland.

Distributed in the United States by North-South Books Inc., New York.

Library of Congress Cataloging-in-Publication Data is available.
A CIP catalogue record for this book is available from The British Library.

ISBN 0-7358-1045-1 (TRADE BINDING)
1 3 5 7 9 TB 10 8 6 4 2
ISBN 0-7358-1046-X (LIBRARY BINDING)
1 3 5 7 9 LB 10 8 6 4 2
Printed in Belgium

For more information about our books,
and the authors and artists who create them,
visit our web site: http://www.northsouth.com

Contents

1. A Storm at Sea

Outside, a storm was raging. Wind rattled the roof tiles. Rain clattered against the windows. Black clouds raced across the sky.

Indoors everything was dark, as dark as dusk, though it was only midday. Paul and his parents were eating their lunch by candlelight. The storm had cut off their electricity. The telephone was dead too.

"I certainly wouldn't want to be out in this weather!" said Paul's father.

He meant out at sea. Paul's father was a fisherman, and no fisherman would go to sea in weather like this. "That would be asking for trouble," Paul's father said.

Paul stared
at his empty plate.
"If only I had a dog,"
he said sadly.

"What made you think of that out of the blue?" asked his father.

"I don't know," said Paul. "I just really want a dog. I'd call him Johnny."

Paul looked at his father hopefully. "I'm almost nine now," he said. "That's old enough to have a dog, don't you think?"

But Paul's father shook his head. "You can't just walk into a shop and buy a dog as if it was a new toy," he said. "You have to prove yourself worthy."

Paul didn't really understand what being worthy meant, and his father didn't explain.

As Paul was clearing the table, heavy footsteps clumped up the steps to the front door. Their friend Alex appeared in the doorway. "A fishing boat is in trouble near the rocks at North Point," he said breathlessly. "She'll go down with all hands unless we get to her, fast."

Alex, Paul's father, and a few other men from the village were volunteers who manned the lifeboat in emergencies. They always had to be ready to help sailors in danger, even in the middle of the night, or in stormy weather like this.

Paul's father jumped up. Paul's mother got out his coat and boots. She gently brushed her husband's cheek with her hand.

"We'll have to haul the lifeboat over the dunes on the cart," said Alex. "It's the only way."

The door banged shut behind him.

A gust of wind made the candle flames
flicker, and ghostly shadows flitted across
the wall.

Paul's mother bowed her head. Her lips were moving, but she made no sound. Paul knew she was saying a silent prayer.

2. Across the Dunes

"Can I go with them?" Paul asked quietly. "Just to watch them haul the boat over the dunes?"

Paul's mother looked up. For a moment it seemed she hadn't heard his question, but then she nodded and said, "Yes, but only across the dunes. Not a step further, do you understand?"

Paul ran outside.

A squall swept across the beach, and the wind whipped the rain at him, stinging his face. Water ran down his neck, inside his scarf. It flowed down his back in an icy stream, but Paul ignored it. He fought his way forward, gasping for breath.

When Paul arrived at the boathouse, the horses were already harnessed to the cart.

The men's faces looked grim and determined. They hardly spoke. All of them knew what they had to do.

Big Larsen urged the horses on. Paul's
father, Alex, and the other men leaned
against the back of the cart and pushed with
all their might. Paul pushed too, until his
legs felt weak.

Slowly and painfully they inched through
the deep sand, while the storm hurled itself
against them, forcing them back. Big Larsen
tugged the reins, urging the horses on:
"Come on, you big softies! You can do it,
my beauties!"

At last they reached the top of the dunes, and the sea lay below them, dark and seething.

Farther out, breakers thundered against sharp rocks.

Plumes of spray shot high in the air. Waves pounded the fishing boat, tossing it dangerously close to the rocks.

On the battered bridge, two figures clung
desperately to the rails, shouting for help.

Big Larsen gave one final heave, and
dragged the horses into the surf.

The men now stood knee deep in icy
water as wave after wave threatened to
knock them off their feet.

When the horses felt the lifeboat lift off
their cart, they whinnied and raced back
onto the dunes.

The horses snorted and stamped. They were still terrified. Paul patted them on the neck, trying to calm them.

The men clung grimly to the outside of the lifeboat. Then Paul's father heaved himself on board. The others followed.

The lifeboat struggled to the crest of a wave, then vanished into the next trough. Paul held his breath until he saw the boat once again, bobbing among the breakers.

3. Just in the Nick of Time!

"Go home, lad!" Big Larsen bellowed in Paul's ear. "You don't want your feet to get as cold as mine!"

But Paul stood and stared into the wind, until his eyes watered so much that he could hardly see. When Big Larsen handed him a mug of hot tea, Paul sipped it gratefully, but he never took his eyes off the lifeboat.

Look! There it was! For a brief moment the lifeboat came alongside the wreck, in the trough between two waves. One of the sailors jumped.

"They've got him!" yelled Big Larsen, clapping Paul on the shoulder. "They've got him!"

The lifeboat pulled away before another swell could smash it against the hull of the fishing boat.

The lifeboat slid back, along a crest of foam. Another man jumped from the fishing boat's wheelhouse, but he fell short of the lifeboat!

The crashing waves closed over the man's head. He surfaced again and . . .

Yes! They had him too!

The lifeboat ventured back again and again, until all of the fishing boat's crew were safely on board.

"Good job, boys!" Big Larsen shouted into
the wind, and at last he let go of Paul's
shoulder, which he had been squeezing hard.
"Come along," he said. "There's work for us
to do."

"But look!" Paul said. He pointed at the wreck. "There's still someone on the fishing boat."

"Nonsense," said Big Larsen.

"It's a dog!" Paul shouted. "They've left a dog behind on the wreck!"

"Can't be helped," said Big Larsen. "Come on."

He drove the horses back into the surf, to collect the lifeboat.

"Dad!" shouted Paul, the moment the men set foot on the beach. "Dad, you've left a dog behind on the wreck. You forgot the dog!"

"I know," said his father, hugging him, "but we couldn't get any closer. We had taken enough risks already. We got the people off. That's the main thing. Now run home and tell Mother we're coming. We have to get these people warm."

4. Jump!

But Paul didn't go home. Instead he took the path to the rocks. Even here, on the far side of the dunes, he thought he could hear the dog howling.

When the tide turns, he said to himself, I might get far enough out . . .

The wind seemed to have dropped slightly.

Jagged rocks were starting to show above the water, almost as far out as the fishing boat! Paul climbed carefully across the rocks. His rubber boots kept slipping on the wet surface. But he could see the dog quite clearly now.

Paul could go no further. He was close, but still not close enough! If the dog jumps, he thought, and the next wave carries him towards me, I could probably grab him.

Paul crawled onto a flat rock. Waves washed over its smooth surface, but he had to take the risk.

"Jump!" he urged the dog, but the dog didn't hear. Paul stood up and cupped his hands, like a megaphone. "Jump!" he yelled. "Come on, jump!"

The dog hesitated. It sat back on its haunches and howled.

"Jump!" Paul shouted again.

And suddenly the dog jumped high over
the rail. There was a splash. The dog paddled
for its life. The next wave tossed it at the
jagged rocks.

Paul leaned far out. The collar . . . yes, he had it! He gripped it tightly, but the dog was heavy, and the rock was slippery and wet.

Paul's free hand clung to the edge of the
rock, but he was starting to slip . . .

Suddenly something jerked him back.

Strong hands held him, and grabbed the dog.

They were safe!

"That was close!" gasped Paul's father. "If Larsen hadn't seen you come this way . . ."

He looked angry.

Now I'm in trouble, thought Paul, but his father just hugged him, very tight.

Paul's father picked up the shivering dog and carried him carefully back across the rocks. He told Paul to walk to keep himself warm.

When the men from the village came to meet them and asked if they could help, Paul's father told them, "He needs to keep moving."

So Paul walked, although his legs felt too weak to carry him, and his eyes would hardly stay open.

Paul couldn't remember how he got to bed that night. He had only a dim memory of his mother rubbing him dry with a towel and pouring mug after mug of hot tea down his throat.

He must have fallen asleep after that.

5. Johnny

Paul didn't wake up until a rough tongue licked his hand. He slowly opened his eyes. A dog was sitting next to his bed.

The dog pricked up its ears and tilted its head to one side as if to ask: "Is everything all right?"

"Everything's fine, Johnny," said Paul, and he patted the dog's neck.

Paul rubbed his face against the dog's cold
nose. "Johnny," he whispered, "my Johnny."

Then Paul heard loud voices from the living room. Chairs were pushed back, and heavy footsteps came towards him. His father appeared in the doorway, and behind him stood the crew from the wrecked fishing boat.

Oh, no! They want their dog back,
thought Paul. Of course this wasn't his dog!
He fought back tears as the dog huddled
close to him.

"The ship broke up an hour ago," Paul's father said. "If you hadn't been there, the dog wouldn't have had a chance. So the crew have decided you can keep him."

Paul couldn't believe it. He stared at his father in confusion.

"The dog is yours, Paul. Mother and I have agreed. You have shown yourself worthy of him."

"If you want him, that is," said one of the fishermen, with a shy smile.

"Of course I want him!" cried Paul, and he gave his father a huge hug. "Thank you!"

The dog jumped up and barked, as if it understood every word.

"What's his name?" Paul asked the fishermen.

They shrugged.

"Johnny, of course," said Paul's father. "What else could it be?"

About the Author

Wolfram Hänel was born in Fulda, Germany, and now lives in Hamburg. He also spends time in a small village in Ireland, called Kilnarovanagh, where he, his wife, his daughter, and their black-and-white dog love to walk along the beach on stormy days. Wolfram Hänel's other easy-to-read books for North-South include *Abby*, *Lila's Little Dinosaur*, *Mia the Beach Cat*, and *The Other Side of the Bridge*.

About the Illustrator

Ulrike Heyne was born in Dresden, Germany. She studied fashion illustration and graphic design in Munich, and worked for many years in advertising agencies. She also taught drawing and painting. Following the birth of her second son, she started to illustrate children's books. Since then she has illustrated many children's books, including *Midnight Rider* and *Horses in the Fog* by Krista Ruepp, both published by North-South Books. Ulrike Heyne lives with her husband in Possendorf, near Dresden.

Other North-South Easy-to-Read Books

Abby
by Wolfram Hänel
illustrated by Alan Marks

Bear at the Beach
by Clay Carmichael

The Birthday Bear
by Antonie Schneider
illustrated by Uli Waas

**The Extraordinary Adventures
of an Ordinary Hat**
by Wolfram Hänel
illustrated by Christa Unzner

Jasmine & Rex
by Wolfram Hänel
illustrated by Christa Unzner

Leave It to the Molesons!
by Burny Bos
illustrated by Hans de Beer

Lila's Little Dinosaur
by Wolfram Hänel
illustrated by Alex de Wolf

**Little Polar Bear and
the Brave Little Hare**
by Hans de Beer

Loretta and the Little Fairy
by Gerda Marie Scheidl
illustrated by Christa Unzner

Meet the Molesons
by Burny Bos
illustrated by Hans de Beer

Melinda and Nock and the Magic Spell
by Ingrid Uebe
illustrated by Alex de Wolf

Mia the Beach Cat
by Wolfram Hänel
illustrated by Kirsten Höcker

Midnight Rider
by Krista Ruepp
illustrated by Ulrike Heyne

More from the Molesons
by Burny Bos
illustrated by Hans de Beer

A Mouse in the House!
by Gerda Wagener
illustrated by Uli Waas

On the Road with Poppa Whopper
by Marianne Busser & Ron Schröder
illustrated by Hans de Beer

The Return of Rinaldo, the Sly Fox
by Ursel Scheffler
illustrated by Iskender Gider

Rinaldo on the Run
by Ursel Scheffler
illustrated by Iskender Gider

Rinaldo, the Sly Fox
by Ursel Scheffler
illustrated by Iskender Gider

Spiny
by Jürgen Lassig
illustrated by Uli Waas

The Spy in the Attic
by Ursel Scheffler
illustrated by Christa Unzner

The Upside-Down Reader
by Wilhelm Gruber
illustrated by Marlies Rieper-Bastian